Odd Fish!

Written by Fiona Undrill

Collins

T0321817

We can go deep.

Odd fish are deep down.

This fish looks as if it has feet!

5

This fish is well hidden.

Look for its fin.

We go deeper.

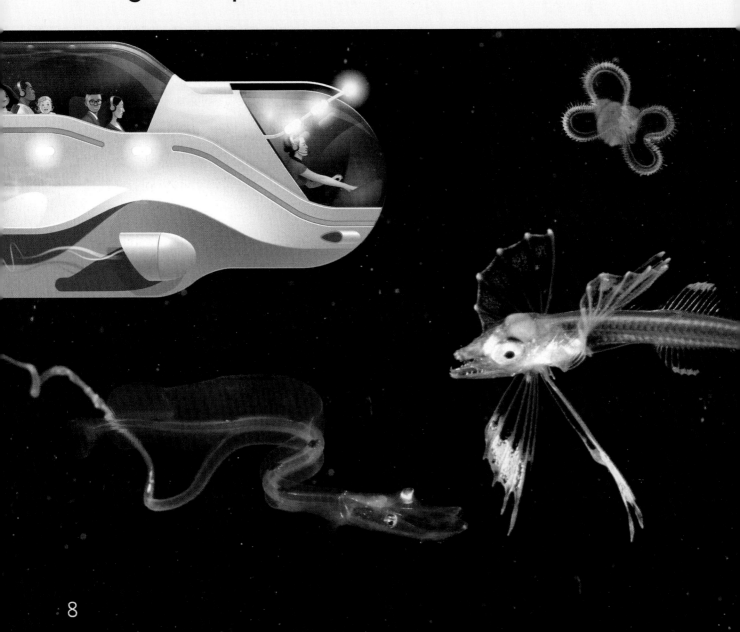

It is as dark as night.

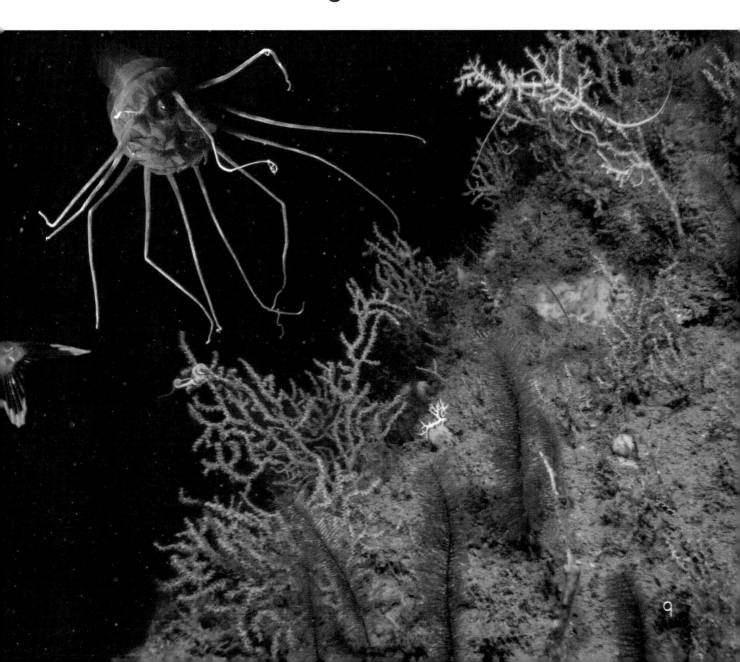

This fish has a light.

It winks in the dark.

This is a goblin shark.

It lurks at the bottom.

Look down deep!

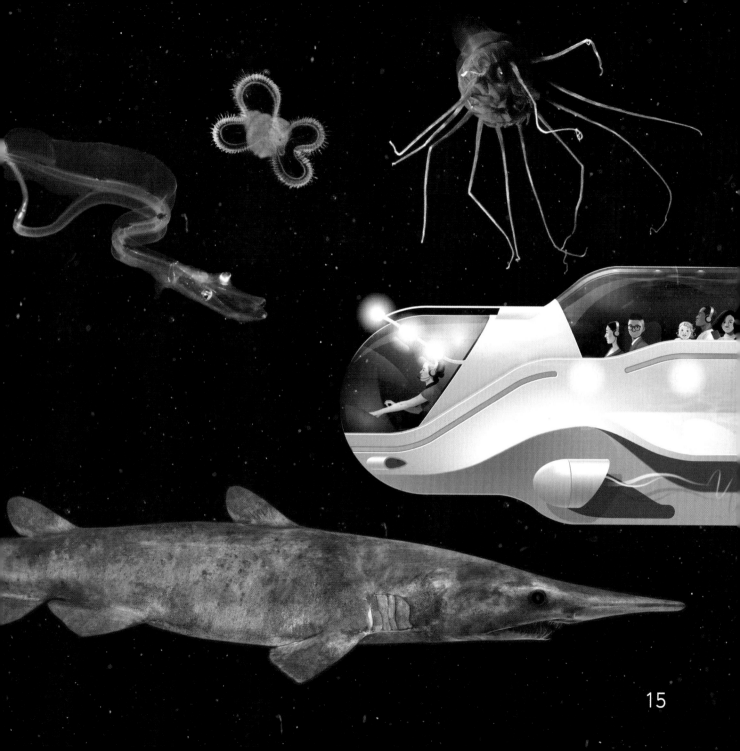

After reading

Letters and Sounds: Phase 3

Word count: 55

Focus phonemes: /ee/ /igh/ /oo/ /ar/ /or/ /ur/ /ow/ /er/

Common exception words: we, go, are, the

Curriculum links: Understanding the world

Early learning goals: Reading: read and understand simple sentences; use phonic knowledge to decode regular words and read them aloud accurately; read some common irregular words.

Developing fluency

- Challenge your child to read the text with authority and enthusiasm, as if they are a wildlife expert taking people on a deep sea tour. If your child stumbles over any words, suggest they reread the sentence.

Phonic practice

- Remind your child that two letters can stand for one sound. Ask your child to sound out, then blend these words:

  d/ee/p   d/ow/n   l/oo/k/s   d/ee/p/er   l/ur/k/s

- Can your child find a word on page 10 in which three letters make one sound? (l/igh/t)

Extending vocabulary

- Take turns to turn to a page and describe the fish. Challenge your child to think of as many words and phrases to describe it as possible, e.g.:
  - pages 10–11 *ugly, round, big mouth, sharp teeth, spikes on its head, dark, bulging eyes*
  - pages 12–13 *long and thin, sharp snout, lots of fins, triangular tail, blotchy, black eyes*

Comprehension

- Turn to pages 14 and 15. Ask your child to use the photos as prompts to describe the journey down to the bottom of the sea.

- On pages 4–5, does this fish have feet? How do you know? (*It doesn't because the author only says it looks as if it has.*)